For Dad and Della

First published 2019 by Walker Books Ltd, 87 Vauxhall Walk, London SE11 5HJ

This edition published 2020

2 4 6 8 10 9 7 5 3 1

© 2019 Daisy Hirst

The right of Daisy Hirst to be identified as author and illustrator of this work has been asserted by her in accordance with the Copyright, Designs and Patents Act 1988

This book has been typeset in WB Natalie Alphonse

Printed in China

British Library Cataloguing in Publication Data: a catalogue record for this book is available from the British Library

ISBN 978-1-4063-9097-1

www.walker.co.uk

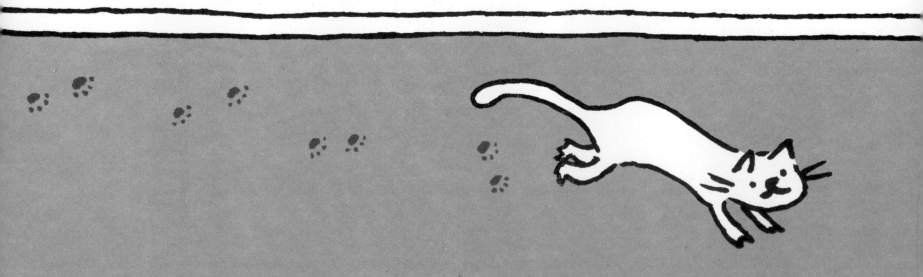

ALPHONSE, THERE'S MUD ON THE CEILING!

Daisy Hirst

WALKER BOOKS
AND SUBSIDIARIES
LONDON • BOSTON • SYDNEY • AUCKLAND

NATALIE and ALPHONSE
lived in a flat.

They had a double-decker
bed to drive,

and the big
green chair
to be quiet
behind

or leap out from, roaring.

There were sunflowers to water
on the balcony,

almost enough space for
roly-polies in the hall,

and a cupboard which seemed to
CLICK and ROAR.

Then Dad got the hoover out
and Alphonse discovered,
"A wild beast's cave!
With sleeping bags!"

"It doesn't look very wild," said Natalie.

"I'll fetch some jungle," said Alphonse.

"You look like a caterpillar," said Alphonse.

"You look like a wriggly worm," said Natalie. "Let's go out wriggling!"

So they wriggled

and wiggled

and
squiggled

and
squoze.

"Hey!" said Dad.
"My coffee!"

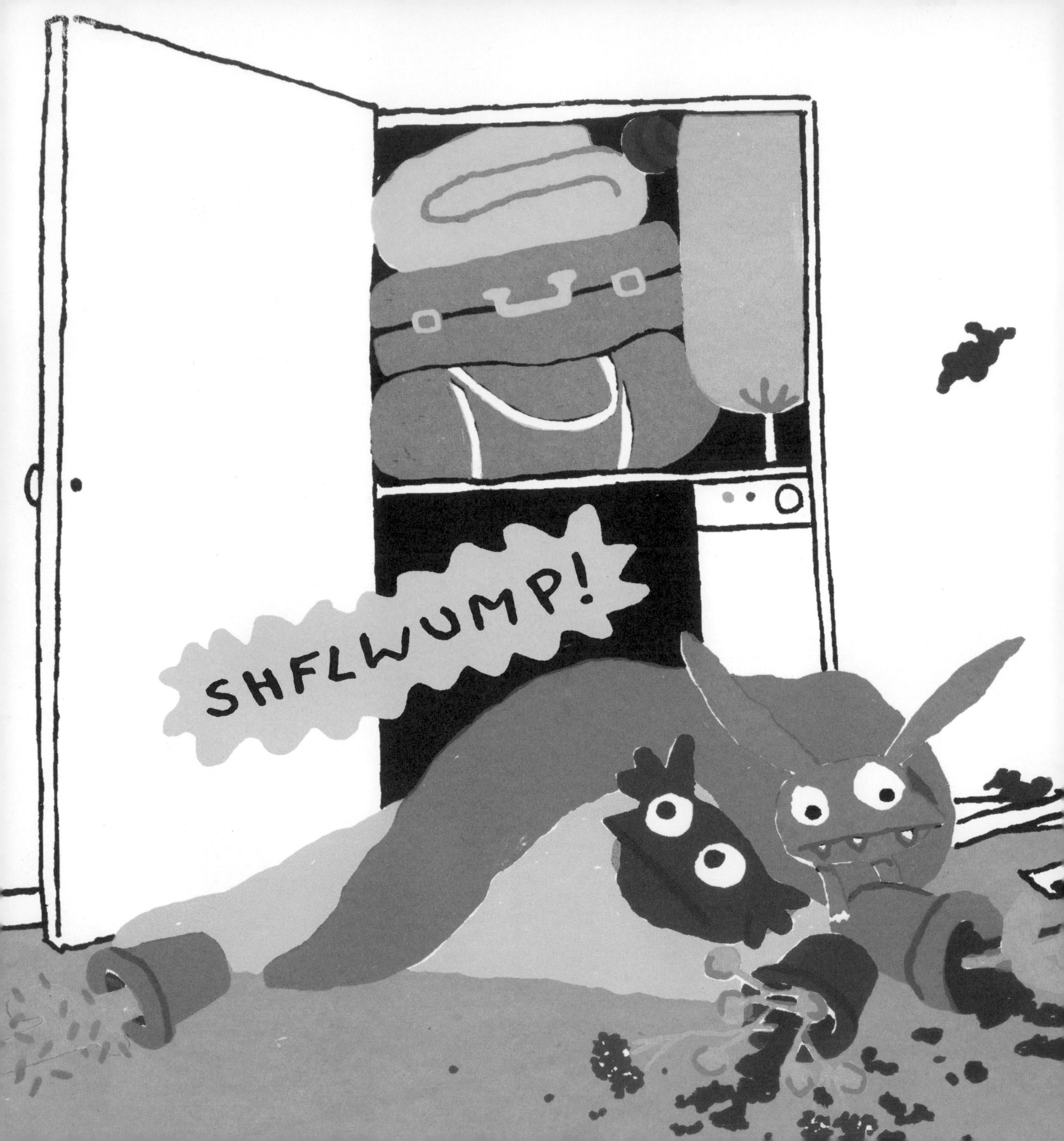
SHFLWUMP!

"OW, ALPHONSE, you're STANDING ON ME!"
said Natalie. "And there's MUD on the CEILING!"

"I'm not standing!" said Alphonse.
"Oh, my sunflower!"

Alphonse cried until his ears hurt.

Dad said, "NATALIEALPHONSE, that is not a good game for indoors!"

Natalie said, "But we only have indoors! Elfrida has a wild jungle garden with a tent in. She's going to really sleep in the tent! Why can't we have a tent in the garden?"

"Well," said Dad, "because we live on the seventh floor."

"I'm going to live in the park," said Natalie.

"Good idea," said Dad. "Let's have an expedition."

"Fine," said Natalie. "But I'm going on my own."

At the park,
Natalie went
exploring.

She found a bush
with a hole in and
crept inside.

Inside the bush, Natalie found a stick, a snail shell and a squirrel. She said, "I will call you Squilliam."

Then Natalie and Squilliam heard rustling.

Who goes there?

"Blackberries!"
said Alphonse.

"Let's live in here,"
said Natalie.

"And eat
blackberries,"
said Alphonse.

"Or you could come home and eat sausages AND blackberries," said Dad.

"On the balcony?" said Natalie.

"OK," said Dad. "But what do you need all those sticks for?"

"I need sticks too!" said Alphonse.

At home, Natalie and Alphonse made a tent on the balcony with the sticks, a blanket and string.

They ate their tea in the jungle.

Then Alphonse taught Natalie
the frog song, with actions.

"Mum," said Alphonse.
"Can we sleep out here really?"

"PLEASE?" said Natalie.

"Well ... you can have five
more minutes," said Mum.

Natalie and Alphonse got into the tent for five minutes.

Natalie counted three stars, two pigeons and one wild Alphonse.

And then one wild
Natalie was really
sleeping, in a tent,
in a jungle on the
seventh floor.

ALSO BY DAISY HIRST:

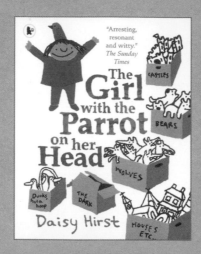

978-1-4063-6552-8

"Arresting, resonant and witty" *The Sunday Times*, Children's Book of the Week

Shortlisted for the Klaus Flugge Prize and the Sheffield Children's Book Award

978-1-4063-7831-3

"A sweet story of an unexpected friendship" *BookTrust*

"An unusual gem of a book, full of charm and humour" *LoveReading4Kids*

Available from all good booksellers www.walker.co.uk